JOVAN
flores

Welcome to Kindergarten

Tim, Come meet your kindergarten teacher on Thursday at 3 o'clock.

Anne Rockwell

Walker & Company • New York

Today is the day—
the day I visit kindergarten!
The school on Sunrise Street is very big.
The boys and girls coming out the door
are all much bigger than me.

Welcome to Kindergarten

A girl waiting by the door
leads us down the hall.

Mrs. Jardin
Kindergarten
Room 1

The kindergarten classroom is very big.

But my mother says it isn't *too* big.

It's just big enough for me

to learn all sorts of things.

The science center is where

I'll learn about things that live and grow.

I'll learn how seeds grow into plants.

INSECTS

by
C. R. Brion

And that's where I'll learn about animals, too—
those that creep and crawl, swim or fly,
and those that run and jump like me.

The art center is where I'll paint pictures
and make things out of wet and squishy clay.

The math center is where I'll learn
to measure and count.
I'll learn about sizes and shapes.

The reading center has lots of books
that I'll learn to read.

One of these tables is where
I'll write with a pencil on sheets of yellow paper
with thin blue lines that are far apart.

The weather center is a felt board
where I will show
whether it's rainy or sunny, hot or cold
when it's my turn to be the weather boy.

One wall has a big, round clock
and I'll learn to tell time on it.
I'll know when it's time to go outside for recess,
time to eat, and time to go home, too.

Fruit and
Vegetables

The cooking center has measuring cups—
bowls, wooden spoons, pots and pans,
and pot holders, too.
That's where I'll learn to mix and measure and cook.

September

SUNDAY	MONDAY	TUESDAY	WEDNESDAY	THURSDAY	FRIDAY	SATURDAY
						1
2	3	4	5 School starts!	6	7	8
9	10	11	12	13	14	15
16	17	18	19	20	21	22
23	24	25	26	27	28	29
30						

**The calendar tells what day of the week
and what month of the year it is.
It tells when I will start going to kindergarten.**

The teacher gives us cookies that this year's
kindergarten class made for us.
A girl named Theresa sits next to me.
She's coming to kindergarten soon—just like me.
She says her sister is already in second grade.

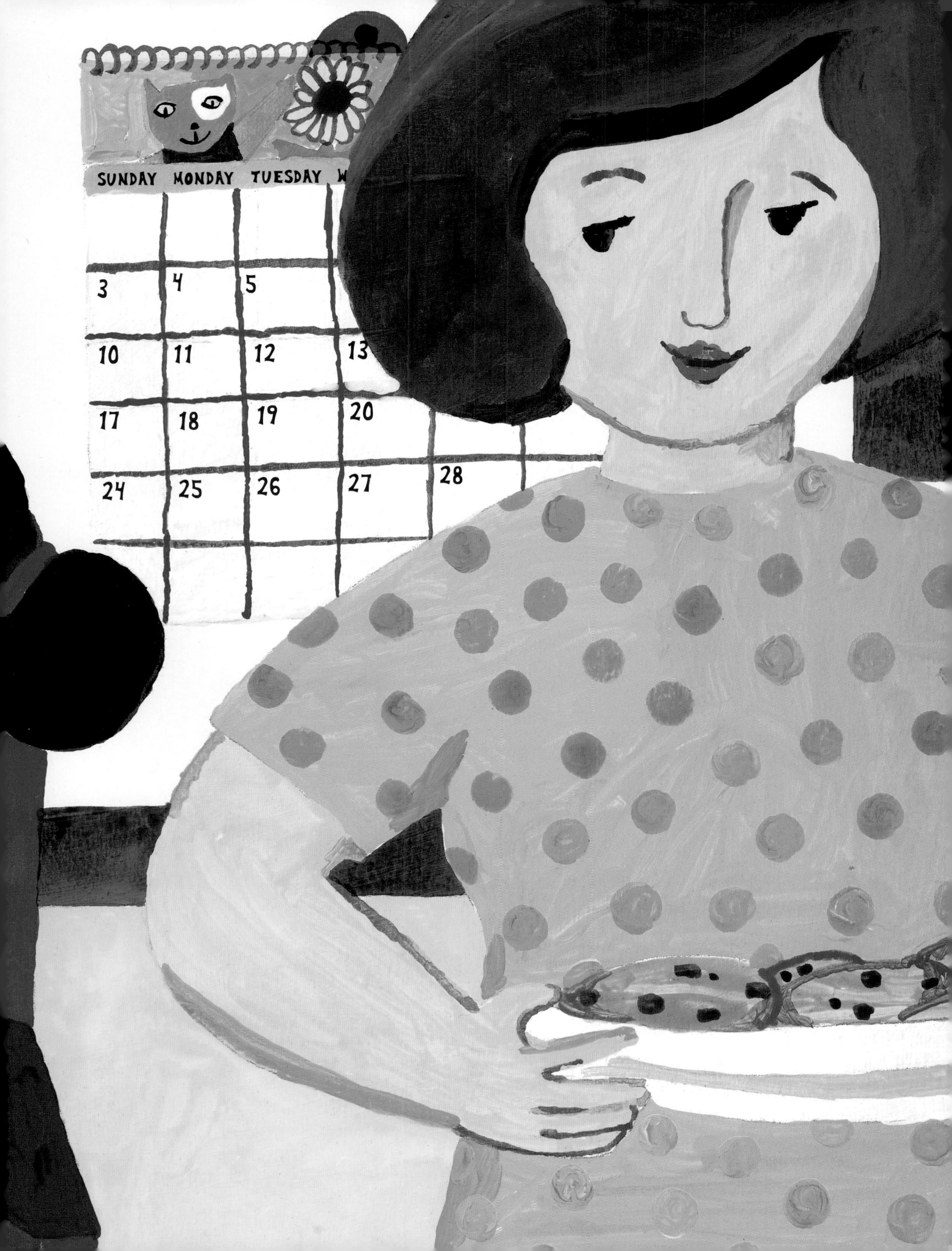
SUNDAY MONDAY TUESDAY
3 4 5
10 11 12 13
17 18 19 20
24 25 26 27 28

When my mother and I walk
down the long hall and out the door—
the building doesn't look too big at all.
It looks just the right size for me!

Welcome

for Christian

First published in the United States of America in 2001 by Walker Publishing Company, Inc.

Published simultaneously in Canada by Fitzhenry and Whiteside, Markham, Ontario L3R 4T8

Library of Congress Cataloging-in-Publication Data
available upon request
ISBN 0-8027-8745-2 (hardcover)
ISBN 0-8027-8746-0 (reinforced)

Book design by Sophie Ye Chin

Printed in Hong Kong

8 10 9